The Wild Bears

By the same author:
BAD MOOD BEAR
THE DREAMBEAST

The Wild Bears

A Red Fox Book

Published by Arrow Books Limited
20 Vauxhall Bridge Road, London SW1V 2SA
An imprint of the Random Century Group

London Melbourne Sydney Auckland
Johannesburg and agencies throughout the world

First published by Hutchinson Children's Books 1989
Red Fox edition 1991

Made and printed in Belgium by
Proost International Book Production

ISBN 0 09 980930 3

The Wild Bears

John Richardson

RED FOX

Before he set off for the day, young Jack Alabaster stood his two teddy bears by the door. 'Keep guard while we are gone,' he said sternly.

But he was being watched. Five wild teddy bears were hiding behind the potting shed; five naughty teddy bears looking for somewhere to live; five *hungry* teddy bears looking for something to eat.

There were Big Bear, Medium Bear, two small bears and a tiny little baby bear called Grub.

As soon as the family had gone, the five wild teddy bears marched straight up to the house and knock, knock, knocked on the big front door.

'You can't come in,' said the two tame teddies.

But those five wild teddy bears marched right inside as bold as can be.

First they went into the kitchen. 'I spy honey!' cried Big Bear. They rubbed their teddy-bear tummies and licked their teddy-bear lips and rolled their teddy-bear eyes as Big Bear reached for the pot.

'You can't do that!' cried the two tame teddies.

'Don't worry,' said Big Bear, 'we won't make a mess.'

But they did. And the little baby bear called Grub made the biggest mess of all.

Next, the five wild teddy bears marched upstairs and straight into Jack Alabaster's very own room.

'Toys!' cried Medium Bear.

'You can't play with those,' screamed the two tame teddies.

'Don't worry,' said Big Bear, 'we won't break anything.'

But they did....

U.S.A.

Then those five wild teddy bears marched straight downstairs, through the hall, out the back door and into the garden.

'Oh, look at these lovely flowers!' cried the two small bears.

'You mustn't pick them,' warned the two tame teddies.

'Don't worry,' said Big Bear, 'we won't pick many.'

But they did. And the tiny little bear called Grub picked every one of Mr Alabaster's prize daisies and hung them round his neck.

'Oh, you naughty bears!' cried the two tame teddies in a fury. But the five wild teddy bears just marched round and round the garden, through the back door, down the hall and up the stairs.

'Bath time,' said Big Bear and in a second the five wild teddies were all in the bath, rubbing and scrubbing and washing their fur and cleaning their ears and scrubbing their backs and splashing water *everywhere*. The two tame teddies had never seen such a mess.

When they were dry the five wild teddy bears made five hot-water bottles and carried them upstairs. Then they got straight into Jack Alabaster's very own bed and fell fast asleep.

'You can't sleep *here!*' cried the two tame teddies. But they could, and they did. And the tiny little baby bear called Grub slept the soundest of all.

But very soon there was a slamming noise and a clicking noise and an opening and a closing. Big Bear awoke with a start. 'They're back!' he cried. And the wild teddies jumped out of bed and ran helter skelter down the stairs and through the hall and out the door and back behind the potting shed.

'Phew!' said Big Bear.
'Phew!' said Medium Bear.
'Phew!' said the two small bears together.
But the tiny little baby bear called Grub said nothing at all. *For he wasn't there!*

From downstairs, Grub heard Mr Alabaster cry, 'Just look at my garden. Who's been picking my flowers?'

'It wasn't us,' said the two tame teddies. But nobody heard.

'And who's been eating the honey?' cried Sophie Alabaster from the kitchen.

'And who's been bathing in the bath and splashing water *everywhere*,' said Mrs Alabaster.

'Oh dear, oh dear, oh dear,' sighed the two tame teddies.

And very, very close to Grub, Jack Alabaster cried, 'Somebody's broken my space rocket!' Then he looked sternly at the two tame teddies. 'I thought I asked you to keep guard,' he said.

'It was those five wild teddies,' said the two tame bears. But their teddy-bear voices were too small to be heard.

That night Jack woke up suddenly. There was a creaking noise, then, to his amazement, he saw the toy cupboard open and a small dark shape scamper across the room to the window and climb out.

He leapt out of bed just in time to see five small shadows at the bottom of the ivy. And, in the light of the moon, the five small shadows turned into five wild teddy bears.

'So *that's* who broke my space rocket!' gasped Jack.
'And picked the flowers and ate the honey and flooded the bathroom,' said the two tame teddies. 'And we *couldn't* make them stop.'

As they watched from the window, the five wild bears ran across the lawn towards the forest.

'And don't come back!' shouted the two tame teddies.

'Don't worry, we won't,' said the tiny little baby bear called Grub.

And they never did.

THE END